An **Andrex** Publication

PUPPY GOES TO PETS DAY

Written by
Gerald Durrell

Illustrated by Cliff Wright

Where I live with Nick and Susan, Mum, Dad and Grandad, it's Grandad who does the gardening.

One day, Grandad started to dig holes in the flowerbed and drop seeds into them. That looks fun, I thought, so I went to the other end of the flowerbed and I started digging too. I can use both my front feet and I'm a really good digger. I had dug quite a lot of holes before Grandad noticed.

"What on earth are you doing, Puppy?" he asked. "You've just dug up all the seeds I planted yesterday. Now I'll never know which plant is which. They'll be a real mixture!" He laughed.

Next, Grandad went to turn the hose pipe on. I love the hose. When the water runs down inside, it wriggles like my friend Grass Snake who lives in the hedge. And when the water comes out it makes a great hissing noise, like Grass Snake when he's angry.

The hose was quite far away from where the seeds had to be watered. So I tugged the end of the hose and started to pull it towards the flowerbed.

"Puppy," called Grandad. "What are you doing now?" He gave me such a surprise that I forgot I had the hose in my mouth.

I turned my head to look at Grandad and the jet of water turned too. Some of it hit Grandad in the tummy - Splosh! - making him sit down - Plonk! He was really wet! We both were! He sat there shaking himself and I shook myself as well. I didn't mind the water.

Then Nick and Susan got back from school and Nick said, "Puppy, it's a special day tomorrow. It's Pets Day at school, and the best pet gets a prize."

I was so excited, I rushed down to the garden hedge to tell my friend Blackbird.

"I wish I could come with you," he sighed, "but these babies of mine take so much feeding I just don't have time."

"How many babies have you got?" I asked, for his nest was high up and I couldn't see into it.

"Five this year," he said gloomily. "They keep you busy, I can tell you. It's worms all the time. And if it's not worms, it's blackberries or red currants or cherries. Still, they're nearly old enough to fly now, and they can go and find their own food. See you soon, Puppy."

And with that, he flew off.

Next morning after Nick and Susan gave me a good wash, we set off in the car.

There was food on the tables in the big pink and white tent and in another tent there were pets in baskets, and aquariums with fish and water pets in them.

Outside that were two pens made out of bales
of straw with pigs, goats and sheep inside. Ducks
and geese were swimming on a big plastic pond,
while a hose pipe kept the water clean.
The ponies and donkeys were in another place.
And of course there were other dogs and cats.

I went into the pets' tent and saw the goldfish swimming around in a big bowl. I jumped up to see them better and nearly knocked the bowl over. The water sloshed everywhere. "Look out!" they said. "We were nearly on the floor."

"Do you always live in round bowls?" I asked. "It must be very boring."

"Of course not," said one of them in a tinkly sort of way. "These are our visiting bowls for going out to places. Our real home is at the bottom of our garden in a pond with water lilies and waterweed. We have all sorts of neighbours like the whirligig beetles who go round and round and never get dizzy.

"And then there are the toads. They live on land, but they come to our pond to lay their eggs. Of course, it's Frog who has been there the longest. Frog and the toads are next to us."

I trotted off to talk to Frog. He was green and black and as shiny as if he had been polished.

"Isn't this exciting?" I asked.

"No it isn't," said Frog. "It's all very boring. I'm next to these awful toads and they keep puffing up their chests and talking about themselves!"

I tried puffing up my chest, but just ended up panting!

A big bell rang and everyone went to get some food. On the way I met a Pekinese called Chang, whose family came from China a long time ago. Nick came over and put a plate of biscuits in front of us, but before we could even start on them, a Bulldog called Terror came along.

"Those are my biscuits," he said. "Give them to me."

"No," shouted Chang, "they're Puppy's and mine."

"I'll show you whose they are," said Terror and
he picked up Chang by the scruff of his neck, shook
him and sent him sprawling.

"Ouch," cried Chang, "that hurt!"

So I leapt at Terror and bit him on the nose, while Chang, who is rather short, bit him on the ankle. People started shouting and telling us off and all three of us were thrown out of the tent by the Headmaster.

Terror got into the most trouble because it was his fault.

Suddenly there was a noise from the straw pens where the sheep, goats and pigs were.

"Help, help," the goats were bleating. "Fire!"

"Help, help - or we'll be roast lamb and pig!" shouted the others.

Chang and I rushed over and we saw in a moment what had happened. Chang thought that somebody had thrown away a match without making sure it was really out and one of the bales of straw was in flames.

I rushed off to find Nick and Susan, past the pond with the ducks and geese. I went flying as I tripped over the hose pipe and landed on my nose. Bump! Then I remembered Grandad in the garden. It had been fun to play with the hose and if it made Grandad wet, it would wet the fire too.

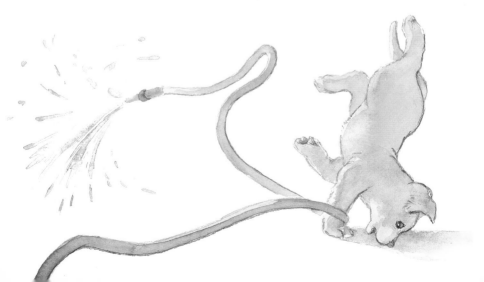

Chang rushed off to the big tent and I dragged the hose from the pond. It kept wrapping around my legs and I nearly fell over, but I got it to the fire and let the water spray about.

Chang was barking and I knew he would be pulling at Nick to make him come. I tried to hang on to the hose but my face and whiskers, and even my ears, were beginning to feel quite hot. Then a voice shouted, "Fire! Fire!" and everyone came running. Nick took the hose from me and people came rushing with buckets of water. Soon the blaze was out without anyone getting hurt...
except for my whiskers.

Then the Headmaster said, "Puppy, you have saved us all, you and Chang. You are very brave and as a reward I'm going to give you both first prize in the pets' competition."

Wow! Me a hero! (And Chang of course.)

When we went home, I rushed off to see my friend Blackbird. I told him about the day, and all about Terror and the fire. He could see my frazzled whiskers, so he knew I'd been very brave.

"Yes," said Blackbird, "you're a real hero." And he flew back to his family.

hen Blackbird said that, I glowed like
my whiskers - which still felt warm. Then
I yawned. It had been a long day, but I felt
great when I trotted in for a cuddle and bed.